Belonging

Jeannie Baker

WALKER BOOKS

AND SUBSIDIARIES

LONDON · BOSTON · SYDNEY · AUCKLAND

First published 2004 by Walker Books Ltd
87 Vauxhall Walk, London SE11 5HJ

This edition published 2007

12 14 16 18 20 19 17 15 13 11

© 2004 Jeannie Baker

The right of Jeannie Baker to be identified
as author/illustrator of this work has
been asserted by her in accordance with the
Copyright, Designs and Patents Act 1988

This book has been typeset in Garamond

The artwork was prepared as collage constructions
which were reproduced in full colour from
photographs by Andrew Payne

Printed in China

British Library Cataloguing in Publication Data:
a catalogue record for this book is available
from the British Library

ISBN 978-1-4063-0548-7 (paperback)
ISBN 978-1-4063-0941-6 (big book)

www.walker.co.uk

Find out more about Jeannie Baker's books
by visiting her website: www.jeanniebaker.com

Thank you to all my friends who helped,
especially Beth, Barbara, Jasmin, Susan,
Henri, Haydn and David

On Your
Wedding

♡

Throughout the world, most people live in cities or urban communities and don't feel a strong connection with the land on which they live. Often people think they own the land — that it belongs to them as a thing, a possession.

But, at the same time, we depend completely on the land to feed us and support us and inspire us. And so we can see that it is the other way around: we belong to the land. If we keep it healthy, it will sustain the web of life on which we depend.

In some cities, communities are working to bring back the variety of local native plants and animals that once lived there. People are discovering the need to nurture and be nurtured by the unique character of the place where they live.

It takes time, as this book shows. But by understanding the land on which we live and by caring for it we can choose between just having a place to live or belonging to a living home.